The Magic Key

Nadim's Machine

OXFORD
UNIVERSITY PRESS

The children were playing with Robark, the robot dog, when suddenly he started running backwards and crashed into Dad.

'Why can't that wretched robot look where he's going?' Dad muttered.

'Because he does everything backwards,' replied Chip.

'It's the way Nadim put him together,' said Wilma.

Nadim needed to fix Robark, before he caused any more trouble! Wilf grabbed the instructions.

'I don't need the instructions,' said Nadim, as he got out his screwdriver.

'Yes you do, Nadim,' cried Wilf. 'Why won't you do what you're supposed to?'

I wish he would, thought Floppy. Before someone gets hurt. The key on Floppy's collar started to glow.

Wilf, Nadim, and Floppy were pulled into a vortex of sparkling colours and lights. They were flying round and round, faster and faster . . .

They landed in the middle of a huge toy factory.

'Cool!' said Nadim, looking round at all the machines.

Suddenly they heard a booming voice shouting, 'Get on with it, Grubbytech!'

They decided they'd better hide.

They could see a man in a smart suit giving orders.

'The sooner you turn those elves into robots, the sooner they can make the toys that make me rich!' he shouted.

Wilf and Nadim looked at each other in alarm. Turn elves into robots? This place should come with a serious elf warning, thought Floppy.

They watched in horror as Grubbytech began turning dials and flicking switches. There was a flash of light and the elves were transformed into robots.

Grubbytech grinned. 'Robotization complete, sir!' he said.

Then he flicked another switch and all the robot elves started work.

'Bang with a hammer – bang, bang, bang!

To make Grabber Lotterdosh a very rich man!' they sang.

'Those poor elves!' said Nadim. 'There must be something we can do!' And he ran into a huge machine, with Floppy and Wilf close behind.

Nadim stared at all the buttons, switches, and monitors. He peered at one screen and said, 'We're in robot mode.'

Wilf was getting nervous. 'I think we should get out of here,' he said, and he and Floppy edged towards the door.

But Nadim was still looking at the screens. 'It looks as if there's a machine mode too,' he said. 'So why are they robotizing the elves?'

It didn't make sense.

Meanwhile, Grubbytech's computer had detected intruders.
'SPIES!' roared Grabber Lotterdosh. 'Don't just stand there – find
them!'

Nadim was determined to find a way of derobotizing the elves. He pulled a lever . . .

'Emergency, emergency!' cried the robot elves. Nadim had brought the conveyer belt to a complete stop.

'We've got to get out of here NOW!' cried Wilf.

Wilf and Floppy ran out of the machine, but it was too late. Grabber Lotterdosh and Grubbytech had spotted them.

They put them into seats by the robot elves.

'What are you going to do?' asked Wilf in terror.

'Robotize! Robotize! Robotize the spies!' chanted the elves.
Grubbytech pulled a lever and . . .

BOOM! Wilf and Floppy had been turned into robots!

Nadim was still inside the machine. He stared at the computer screen in disbelief as he saw what was happening to his friends.

'Where is the derobotizer?' he wailed. 'There must be some instructions somewhere.'

Then he spotted them. He looked at the diagrams carefully – if he could just get this to work . . .

Wilf and Floppy were busy working with the elves.
'Robot elves both young and old,
   Making toys the way we're told,' chanted Wilf and the elves. Even
Floppy whined along in rhythm!

Nadim had worked out the instructions! He pressed a red button, turned a dial, flicked a switch, then pulled the big red lever . . . There was a loud bang and lots of flashing lights.

The derobotization had worked!

The elves jumped up and down with joy. Wilf blinked, and then set to work unstrapping himself and Floppy.

'Who derobotized my elves?' cried Grabber.

'I did, sir,' said Nadim, appearing from the machine. 'You won't ever need to robotize any elves ever again. The machine can do all the work without them!'

Nadim showed Grabber and Grubbytech how to work the machine mode, instead of using robots. Grabber was delighted – but not as delighted as the elves!

One of them turned to Nadim and gave him his hat with a grateful bow.

'If you ever want a job, you know where to come,' said Grabber to Nadim.

'Er, thank you, but . . .' began Nadim.

Then Wilf pointed at Floppy.

'The key's glowing,' he cried.

We're going, thought Floppy.

They were all back in the Robinsons' garden.

Nadim picked up Robark's instructions. Maybe he should look at them after all!

It was simple – all he had to do was swap Robark's head and tail around and Robark started working perfectly.

Floppy picked up his bone.

Some dogs are born to be robots, he thought. But he certainly wasn't one of them!

OXFORD
UNIVERSITY PRESS

Great Clarendon Street, Oxford OX2 6DP

Oxford University Press is a department of the University of Oxford.
It furthers the University's objective of excellence in research, scholarship,
and education by publishing worldwide in

Oxford New York

Auckland Bangkok Buenos Aires Cape Town Chennai
Dar es Salaam Delhi Hong Kong Istanbul Karachi Kolkata
Kuala Lumpur Madrid Melbourne Mexico City Mumbai Nairobi
São Paulo Shanghai Taipei Tokyo Toronto

Oxford is a registered trade mark of Oxford University Press in the UK and in certain other countries

British Library Cataloguing in Publication Data available
ISBN 0-19-272449-5
3 5 7 9 10 8 6 4 2
Printed in Great Britain